Harry Kitten and Tucker Mouse

Harry Kitten and Tucker Mouse

by George Selden

Pictures by Garth Williams

Farrar · Straus · Giroux

NEW YORK

For Pat Saffron

and I only wish that

this slender book were as big as

the bond that binds me

to her

G.S.

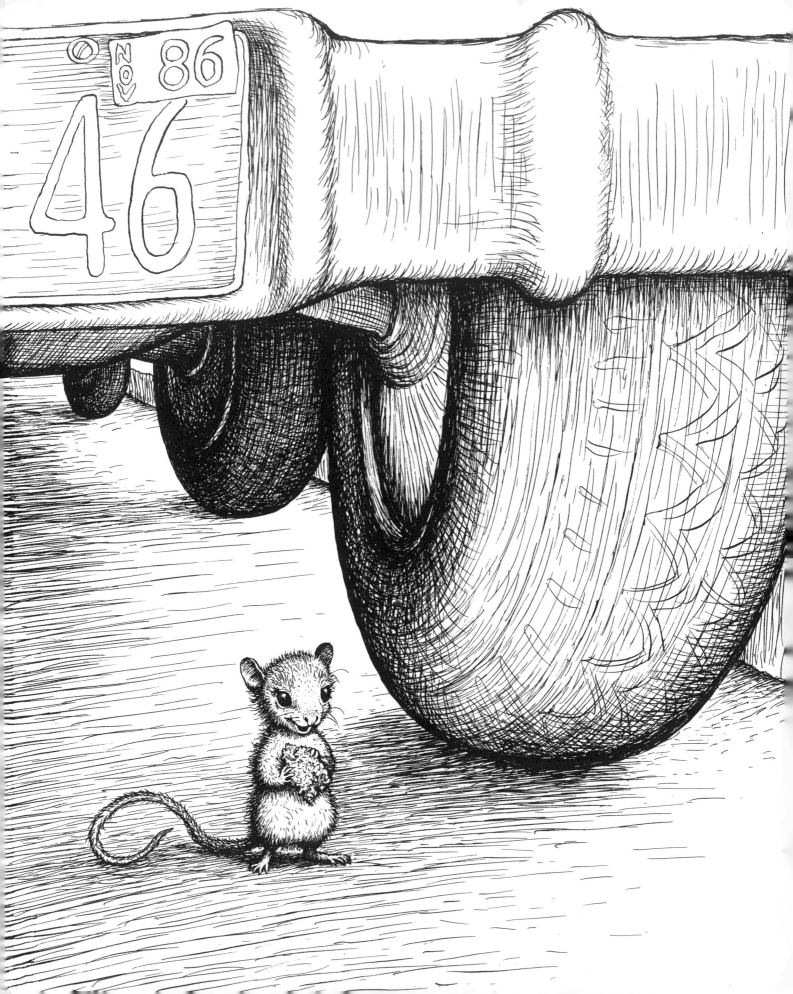

"At least I could have a name!" the tiny mouse said to himself.

He was picking his way, very carefully, along the gutter of Tenth Avenue in New York City. *Whssht!*—just like that, he'd dart from under one parked car to the dark dirty safety beneath another. For this young little mouse had found that the human beings didn't like him much. Some of those two-legged creatures, who thought they owned the whole city, called him a rat—which he definitely was *not*!—when they saw him. And some called him a rodent. And one just said, "Yeck!"—which sounded most unkind of all.

"But at least I can have a name," the mouse said, as

he paused to nibble the crust of a cheese sandwich that one of the human beings had thrown away. He wished there had been more cheese and less crust. "My own name." He quickly hid behind a tire, as a threatening leather boot came near.

"I could be Hamlet. Hamlet Mouse." The night before, in the theater district, the young mouse had heard two human beings, very well dressed, say that they were going to a show called *Hamlet*. "But I don't like 'Hamlet,'" the mouse said to himself. "It sounds too much like a little pig."

There was another possibility. Godzilla Mouse. Two teenage boys were going to a horror movie and the mouse had overheard them talking. "Godzilla Mouse—?"

"It just isn't me," he decided.

But who was he? If he didn't have a name, he wouldn't be anyone. For a name makes a person very special. He is *himself*—and no one else.

A group of young girls walked by the car under which the mouse was hiding.

These laughing young girls—one of them had soft fuzzy hair and a high sweet voice—reminded the mouse of the very first thing that he could remember. That was a nest, made of scraps of cloth, and thrown-away Kleenexes, and other comfortable, cozy odds and ends. And there also was a soft warm furry weight—the word "Mother" rang in his ears—that tried to protect him from pounding shovels, and nasty words, and the threat of death. There were men in uniforms, sanitation workers. And he ran.

He'd run, the young mouse had, and *still* was running.

Since then, there'd been no warmth, no weight, no comforting covering. There had only been darting from one parked car—a temporary refuge—to another.

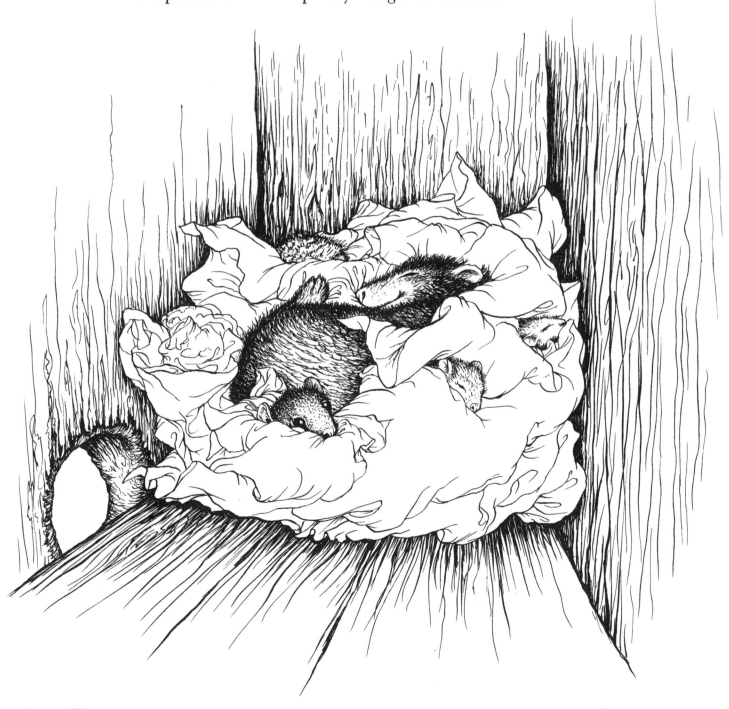

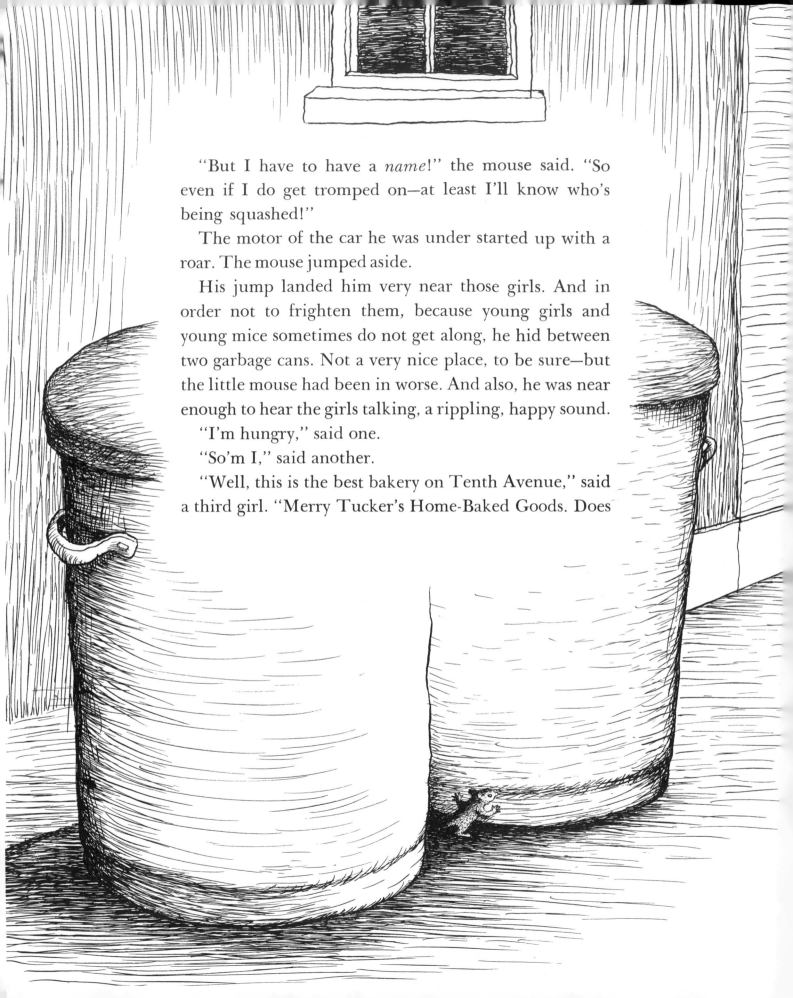

"But I have to have a *name*!" the mouse said. "So even if I do get tromped on—at least I'll know who's being squashed!"

The motor of the car he was under started up with a roar. The mouse jumped aside.

His jump landed him very near those girls. And in order not to frighten them, because young girls and young mice sometimes do not get along, he hid between two garbage cans. Not a very nice place, to be sure—but the little mouse had been in worse. And also, he was near enough to hear the girls talking, a rippling, happy sound.

"I'm hungry," said one.

"So'm I," said another.

"Well, this is the best bakery on Tenth Avenue," said a third girl. "Merry Tucker's Home-Baked Goods. Does

anyone feel like a glazed doughnut or a raspberry tart?
They're to *die* over, they're so good!"

The girls twittered their excitement. And went into
the bakery.

And oh!—a glazed doughnut! A raspberry tart! The
little mouse—whose mouth was now watering—could have
died over either one. But something even more in-
teresting echoed in his ears. *Merry Tucker's Home-
Baked Goods.*

He felt there was something special in those words.
A name!

"It can't be Merry," he said to himself. "Sounds too

11

much like Mary." And if you were going to grow up and be a "he" mouse—well, a name like Mary would just not do.

But Tucker—he mused and repeated the name. "Tucker Mouse." It sounded quite original. Not ordinary like Tom, or Joe, or Bill. "*Tucker* Mouse!" he shouted. "That's me."

The name tasted more sweet and more strong in his mouth than even a raspberry tart.

So, armed with his name, the mouse marched—through the gutter, it's true—but he marched down Tenth Avenue. His name—Tucker Mouse—which he'd looked for so long gave him strength, courage—gave him life!

Tucker Mouse skittered after the girls, darting close
to the buildings that lined the street. He was hoping
that one of the girls might drop a little piece of pastry.
But, sadly, they all liked tarts and doughnuts as much
as he did, and smacking their lips, which made it worse,
not one of them dropped a single crumb.

Then up ahead he saw what he feared most of all in
the world: a garbage truck—and all around it, sanitation

workers scooping up trash from the sidewalk. Tucker Mouse knew that the uniformed men thought he was trash, too. He felt lonely and afraid again.

And tired. So tired. He had to find a place to rest. A narrow, dark alley opened between a tenement and a dry cleaner's. As Tucker was scooting in, he happened to see a small copper coin on the sidewalk. Instinctively, he snatched it up in his two front paws—then vanished into the sheltering dark.

"A penny!" he exclaimed out loud—quite proud that he'd found it, and saved it.

"The human beings think pennies are good luck," said
a voice behind him.

Tucker whirled around. In the dark behind him,
nibbling a crust—the remains of a sandwich—he saw a
kitten. His first thought was: Poor guy! He's as starved

15

as I am. But then he remembered: I am a *mouse*—and this is a kitten, who will very likely become a *cat*.

"Ya wanna fight?" he demanded.

"Why?" The kitten put down his crust, and simply asked, "Why?"

"Well—well—" Tucker Mouse was flustered. "It's just that—well—cats and mice *fight*. That's all."

"But why?" the kitten continued to question. "I was starving to death before I found this pitiful piece of sandwich. Some overfed human being missed that

garbage can, so *I* got to eat. And you don't look too beefy yourself. So why make life worse for each other by fighting?"

Tucker Mouse was somewhat taken aback. He hadn't expected such reasonable talk from a skinny kitten sitting next to a trash can and a decaying pumpkin.

"But—what do we do if we *don't* fight?" asked Tucker.

"Mmm—" The kitten purred softly, like a philosopher. "We could just be friends—"

"*What—?*"

"Not so loud. The human beings are all around."

Tucker nodded ruefully: they were surrounded.

"I know that it's unusual," said the kitten. "At least, I know it's supposed to be. But this is New York! And all the rules are broken here. For the best, I hope. We might even set a precedent—"

"What's a precedent?"

"It's a new way of thinking," said the kitten. "And a new way of feeling, too."

"You promise not to eat me?"

"I will never be *that* hungry." The kitten patted the small mouse's head. "And even if I was—I couldn't. My teeth aren't big enough. Yet."

"Mmm—" The mouse had to think about that. "For a mouse to trust a cat—"

"You've got to trust somebody—sooner or later," the kitten declared. "Why not try me?"

"Well—okay. For a while. But I'm keeping an eye on those teeth!"

Tucker sighed and looked down the alley, where some sanitation workers were doing their job. For a moment he even wished them well. They have problems, too, he thought to himself—but I hope that I am not one of them.

"You want some sandwich?"

18

Tucker Mouse said nothing.

"Come on," urged the kitten. "It's ham-and-cheese.
Mice like cheese—"

19

"Ohhh!" Tucker groaned with delight.

"Then just you munch on this piece. See? There is ham and *also* cheese on this crust."

"I *am* sort of hungry—" admitted Tucker. "But it isn't a raspberry tart."

"Well, listen to the mousiekins!" The kitten purred. "Next time I'll try to supply—"

"Don't you *dare* call me mousiekins!"

"—beef steak. Or corned beef."

"Oh, can I have a bite?" said the mouse. "I'm so *hungry*! You can't believe—"

"It's all yours," said the kitten. "I'm full."

"Full?" The thought of being full of food had never occurred to the mouse before.

"Munch out!" said the kitten.

And Tucker munched.

Between mouthfuls—for there's more to a crust than a human being might think—he asked, "What's your name?"

And then, before the kitten could answer, he explained, between munches, why his name was Tucker.

"Why, that's very much like—it's exactly what happened to me!" said the kitten. And friendship, like a frail tree, grew between them.

"I, too," said the kitten, "was hiding from everybody. I wanted to be invisible—" The kitten sighed. "Although I had always felt I was—well, you know—special."

"Me, too," said Tucker.

"But then two kids walked by." The kitten's voice brightened. "And one had an arm around the other's shoulders—these two nice guys were just talking like friends." The kitten purred at the memory. "And then the one with scraggly blond hair said, 'Harry—you're a *character*!' "

The kitten's eyes blazed at the memory. " 'Harry—you're a character!' the kid said. So I knew that was my name," said the kitten, "since I've always wanted to be a character. And a *character*'s name is Harry!"

The kitten fell silent. Except for a purr, which sounded to Tucker's attentive ears like loyalty and, maybe, trust.

"So I'm Harry," said the kitten.

"And I am Tucker," said the mouse.

A thoughtful silence grew long, and then longer, between them. But outside the private silence they shared were taxis honking, huge trucks roaring—the din and danger of New York.

"So where do we go from here?" asked the mouse, with a tremble in his voice that he tried hard to hide.

Harry thought a moment and then exclaimed: "Oh, I know where! There's a great big building—and it must have *lots* and *lots* of cellars—where we'd be safe. Follow me." He began to creep warily down the street. It was evening now, and he and his friend could slip through the failing light like ghosts.

"Wait! Wait!" shouted Tucker. "I have to hide my penny. When I can, I'm going to come back and get it."

There was a Cadillac nearby, and the mouse thought of shoving it under one wheel. It had been parked there a very long time—the meter said so. But the little mouse reconsidered. If it had been there so long, the police would probably be coming soon to drag it away to the place where cars went to jail until their owners came to claim them.

"Every mouse should have his Life Savings. And this penny is the beginning of mine."

He decided, finally, and after much scuttling back and forth, that it just might be safe wedged between two bricks in the tenement wall that faced the alley. "Now don't let me forget where I've put it."

"I have a suspicion you'll *never* forget," said the kitten.

By now, he'd begun to form an idea of his friend's character. It was—no, not "greedy"—but rather, "acquisitive." Which is much the same thing, but in much nicer terms.

"I am ready," Tucker Mouse announced. "Now where?"

"To the deep and mysterious lower levels of the greatest building in all the world," said the kitten. "The fantastic and fabulous Empire State Building!"

"Oh," mumbled Tucker. "I never heard of it."

Harry made a face—which looked like pity (or maybe disbelief). "Even the meekest mouse," he said, "must surely have heard of the Empire State."

"Well, I haven't," said Tucker. "So show me."

An hour's scurrying, hurrying, worrying—then it rose above them: beautiful and unbelievable.

"They really do know something," said Tucker. "The human beings." He looked up, up. "Just look at that!"

"Let's see what's underground," said Harry Kitten. "I've heard about those cellars ever since I can remember."

"And when is that?" asked Tucker, with a hush in his voice.

"I don't know," said Harry. "The first thing—the really very first thing—I remember is shivering, last month, in a pipe made of iron. There was some cat there —little, like me, with black-and-white fur. Then I forget. But maybe I have brothers and sisters somewhere."

"Show me the building," said Tucker Mouse. He

coughed, because Harry seemed to be dreaming and sad, and Tucker had to interrupt. "And tell me all about, and show me, all the fantastic, fabulous cellars. Underground. Please? Harry? Even if they're scary."

"Okay," said Harry. His voice was still dull. "But I don't know about the lower levels."

"Come on," said Tucker. "Let's adventure."

"We have to go down, and down, and down," said Harry.

The kitten and the mouse prowled carefully around the huge building. And in back they found a freight elevator on the street level that hadn't completely closed. Like two furry, quick blinks—and they almost *were* invisible—they dashed through.

It was eight o'clock, and most of the weary human beings had, gratefully, gone home.

"We're in luck," said Harry. "We can prowl at our leisure."

They jumped down to the floor below. A dark passageway, barely lit by a series of weak white bulbs, stretched endlessly ahead of them.

"We may need a hunk of that stuff, luck," said Tucker, staring into the gloom. "I wish I had my penny."

"Oh, we'll be lucky!" said Harry jauntily. "As you said before: let's do some exploring. Adventuring!"

The stairways—some marked EMERGENCY EXIT—the airshafts, the endless, endless corridors—no one can describe the lower levels of the Empire State Building.

At one point, outside a closed elevator door, Tucker had to stand on Harry's shoulders—even with the help of a nearby ladder—to push the button with an arrow on it that pointed down.

"I suppose that's us," said the mouse, as he weaved and wobbled dangerously, and finally managed to push that button. "There."

The door opened—they entered—nobody there—and the elevator began to descend. And descend. And *descend*!

"Harry—we are coming out in *China*."

"No, we're not. Just wait." The kitten sounded very sure—for someone who wasn't all that sure. At last the elevator stopped. The door opened. Out they ran. "You see, mousiekins—"

"I have asked you not—"

"—the lowest level. That's what the elevator button says. We're here. And get off my shoulders, by the way."

"The lowest level," mused Tucker Mouse. "To think that it should come to this."

"Fewer human beings to worry us." Harry offered his jaunty suggestion as hope. "Anyway—we're here."

Here? Here was a tunnel with white tiles for a floor, and white tiles for a ceiling, and also white tiles for walls. *Here*, in fact, was *all* white tiles—and not even a sanitation inspector in sight.

"There is absolutely no one around," the kitten went on.

"So I've noticed," said Tucker, eyeing the icy-white canyon they were in. "A *ghost* would make this place feel alive."

"Now, now—"

"Now *what?*" squeaked Tucker Mouse. "We are on the bottomest level. And it feels—and it looks—like Dead Man's Gulch."

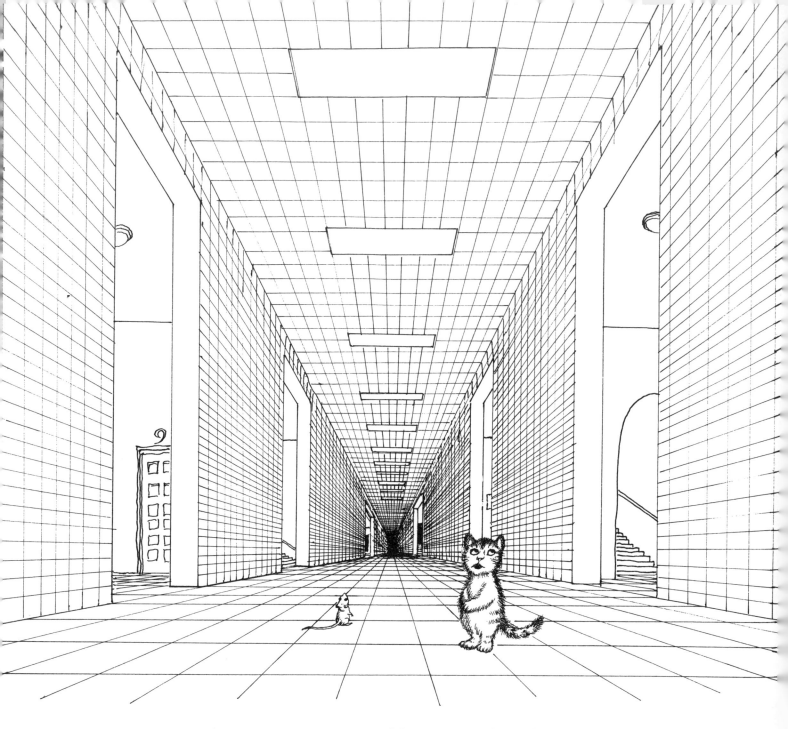

"At the very worst," said Harry, "there is nobody
here—"
"That's just it! *Nobody.*"
"—who would want to do us harm."

28

"At this point," said Tucker, "the chance of a little harm might be quite exciting."

"Shall we take the elevator back up to level four?" asked Harry. "There may be janitors there."

"Let's try it here for a while," said Tucker.

For hours these two—a kitten who wanted to seem very brave and a mouse who was afraid to admit he was scared—roamed through the labyrinth that lies far beneath the Empire State Building.

Now and then they caught sight of men in uniform, the caretakers of the building, who roamed about doing odd jobs—for a building is like a living thing: it needs to be taken care of. That night, there were only a few lonely men. And they were quite easy to avoid.

The solitude, however, the silence and the isolation—they were not so easy to avoid. But still—no one even knew the kitten and the mouse were there.

Food was no problem. The caretakers were very careless. They left little bits of lunches around. A shred of lettuce—a bit of bread—now and then a glob of yogurt in a container.

But lettuce and bread—and even the dregs of old milk shakes are really very dull. If you have too much of them.

"I'd love a hunk of cheese," said Tucker.

"Umm," purred Harry. "Roast beef for me."

The next day came up above. Of course, deep down, they couldn't tell day from night. Tucker looked around, scratched one ear, and said, "Harry, have we been in this particular corridor before?"

"I don't know," said Harry. "They all look alike."

"Precisely!" said Tucker. "That means we are—"

"Don't say it!"

"—*lost*!"

Neither said a word . . .

Then Tucker remembered. "You know—Tenth Avenue wasn't dull. It was very lively, in fact."

"Especially when the sanitation workers were trying to bash you with shovels," said Harry.

"*We've got to get out of here!*" shouted Tucker. "I'm going out of my mind!"

"I agree," said Harry, sighing. "The Empire State Building—beautiful as it is—is not the place for us."

"But we're lost," shrieked Tucker. "And there's no ladder here. Even if we could find an elevator."

There is no more pitiful sight than a young mouse wringing his paws.

"Now, just you wait," said Harry Kitten. And for a kitten, he had learned to speak with a bit of authority. "I have seen something you have *not!*"

"You've seen?" Tucker Mouse talked loudest. But Harry only purred the truth. "What? *What?*"

"I have seen a chalk mark on the wall." Harry, with one paw, pointed to a slender line of chalk that ran along one wall. "We are not the only souls who've been alone down here. One human being also was afraid to get lost. And he'll show us the way out."

"He will?" Tucker couldn't believe his ears.

"He was scared, too. But he had a piece of chalk. And if we follow the line he made—to find his way out—"

"Let's go," yelled Tucker. "Whoever you are—you human being—please save us, too, who are only animals!"

And the chalk line, scribbled on the wall, led Tucker and Harry, as it had that man, to the street.

(The man's name was Matthew. He lived in Queens—which is part of New York—and he had four sons. And the night he drew the chalk line—so he'd know where he had been already—that night was Halloween. And he was on duty—a lucky accident, two years later, for a kitten and a mouse.)

"The street!" said Tucker Mouse and sighed. "Oh, the street."

He was just about to feel relieved when "Watch out!" warned Harry. "Here comes a garbage truck."

"We've got to run—"

"Follow me!" shouted Tucker.

"Follow *you*?"

"I've got brains, too! Maybe little ones—but when I was on Tenth Avenue, just trying to stay alive, I heard some kids say they were going down to the docks to get a suntan."

"The docks?" puffed Harry. He had to run to keep up with his friend. "With all those ocean liners?"

"Not *those* docks," said Tucker. "Down in the lower part of New York there are old, abandoned piers, where people get suntans. If they take their shirt off."

"Old, abandoned piers—"

"Yes. Very run-down. So, safe for us."

"Mmm!" Harry Kitten choked as he ran. "I don't quite like the sound of that."

Furtively, in the late afternoon, the kitten and the mouse made their way to the docks.

And if Harry Kitten didn't like those words—"old, abandoned piers"—he liked the old, abandoned piers themselves much less.

Yet it was sunset, and even in their dangerous ruins the docks, the decaying piers of New York, seemed

almost beautiful. Red and orange light illumined the fallen roofs, the leaning walls. And the everlasting sun —in the west—seemed to bless the place. Behind the two friends, as they sat on the pier, the lights of New York

were flickering on. They, too, as they danced on the great flowing river, seemed like a blessing.

But *nothing* blessed the inhabitants of those piers.

"There are rats here," whispered Tucker.

"Well, you're a—"

"I am a *rodent*, I guess. Not a rat! Not me!" He sleeked down his fur. And gave Harry an appealing smile. "We mice have style." Then he growled ferociously. "And rats have *none*. No style. No niceness. No nothing. The *bums!*"

Tucker looked around. "There are human beings here, too. Look at that guy lying over there, asleep."

"Poor soul," murmured Harry. "I hate to see a human

being so down on his luck. They have to find a place of their own, too."

"I agree." Tucker nodded sympathetically. "I also hate to think of a certain kitten I know—and also a mouse —who are so far down on *their* luck that they have to live here. *Yeck!*"

The "*yeck*" burst out because a frantic cockroach— heaven knows where he was going—had just dashed across Tucker's left paw.

"We'll stay here tonight, and then—*watch out!*"

A crunching, tearing sound came from the ceiling of the pier where they were. Harry yanked Tucker Mouse aside—and a huge chunk of plaster fell just where they'd been sitting.

"If we live through the night," said Tucker, wiping plaster dust off his fur.

"Over here," said Harry. A huge girder had fallen from the roof. There was an open space beneath it. "Get under here. Then, even if more of the roof comes down, we'll be safe."

The two animals crawled beneath the beams.

"Safe," said Tucker. "I've about given up on being safe. Even those kids, with their nice suntans, will probably throw rocks at us tomorrow."

"Well, don't give up on being safe. Rocks and falling beams or not," said Harry. He curled up, and in a few minutes a whizzing, purring, zizzing sound told Tucker that he was asleep.

And after fifteen minutes, so was the mouse. His first dream was all about cheeseburgers.

Next morning, at the very same moment, the two woke up—as if the clocks inside their heads were exactly the same. They were that close.

Dawn gloried over the east. The sight made the great buildings of Manhattan look as if they were dreams. Such great dreams!

"I'm hungry." Tucker yawned.

"We've got no *food.*"

"Oh," Tucker admitted. "Then, what now—"

"I don't know."

And for the first time Tucker heard, not a whimper, but a fearful tone in Harry's voice.

"Come on, Harry," said Tucker Mouse. "If we have to go on looking—we go!"

All that day and night—what with hurrying, scurrying, worrying—the mouse and the kitten made their way uptown. It meant hiding behind fireplugs, in alleys, under cars. And *so* like the old lonely life it was!

The next morning, just at first light—gold streamed from the east—Harry said, "I see green! Look!"

Ahead of them were trees, shrubs, clipped hedges, aglow in the dawn.

"We have to rest here," said Harry.

Heaving sighs of relief and weariness, Harry Kitten and Tucker Mouse crept under an iron fence, through a hedge, and fell asleep.

They woke up together, and on the dot, as usual.

"Just look at these lovely bushes—those trees," said Harry. "Why, it's a protected little park!"

"Protected from *what?*" asked Tucker, who had noticed that, as well as the barred fence around the park, there was a gate. And it was locked. Only the people who lived nearby had a key to get in.

"Oh, you ask so many questions," said Harry.

"I repeat—if this part of New York is so nice—protected from *what*?"

"Oh—from hoodlums and beggars and troublemakers. And also, I would guess, from horrible dogs who aren't on leashes!"

"And from homeless kittens and mice, too, maybe? A park this well kept could make even me feel like a hoodlum."

"I am trying to find us a place to live—"

"All right. Okay. So we'll give it a try. At least it beats the docks."

So, for a while, one kitten and one mouse lived quietly in Gramercy Park. For that's what it was called. *Very* quietly! Because this park in the heart of New York City seemed to have a discreet sort of upper-class hush about it. Not that there weren't children, or older people, just sitting in the sun, but everyone was—

"They're so polite!" said Tucker.

"You'd rather have rats?" asked Harry, who was munching slowly, to make it last, on half a roast-beef sandwich. The meat was perfectly cooked, too: not too rare, but not too well done. It must have come from a very expensive delicatessen. Harry could not imagine how half a roast-beef sandwich could have been dropped and forgotten in Gramercy Park.

"No, I don't want rats," said Tucker Mouse. "But I wouldn't mind a little *action*! Now, give me a chomp on that roast beef." He gobbled furiously.

"Your manners—my word!" Harry murmured disapprovingly.

Tucker almost choked. "Will you listen to King Kitten here! You improve your manners a little bit more —and lick your fur three times a day—with a little luck, you could get adopted by one of those old women who come here and knit all afternoon. Would you like that, kittykins?"

Harry didn't reply.

Yet Gramercy Park was a beautiful place. Tucker couldn't deny it. There were well-tended trees; there were flowers of all different colors: it was as if an over-ripe rainbow had burst and scattered its seeds over Gramercy Park. The lawn was clipped as neat and nice as a new haircut. Clean benches were set here and there. And also, all around the square, there were lovely old buildings, town houses. But there also was that high iron fence. (Of course, animals could get in through the bars —but even the animals, and especially the squirrels, had exquisite manners.)

So Tucker and Harry, whose manners were not that exquisite or refined, had just slipped through the bars and found themselves in a very well mannered paradise.

What little creatures were living there—a few well-bred insects, especially—were all of a very high class. One praying mantis even nodded to Tucker—and that had never happened before. Indeed, it was the very first time in New York—and perhaps anywhere—that a praying mantis had nodded cordially to a mouse.

"This is heaven," said Tucker. "I got smiled at by a bug!"

But heaven—and would anyone believe this?—even heaven itself, for a mouse, has its disadvantages. A mouse gets nervous. Especially when he almost gets run over by a baby carriage.

One afternoon, a wee bit bored by nothing but leisure, and the idle beauty of Gramercy Park, Tucker Mouse ventured out on the sidewalk, just for a change,

and he almost got squashed by a lovely yellow baby carriage which was being wheeled by a nurse in a starched white uniform. The nurse herself looked quite starched, too.

"Harry," said Tucker, when he had returned to the rhododendron bush they were living under, "which would you prefer: to be mashed by a nurse in a stiff uniform or by a bum on the docks?"

"*What?*" asked Harry.

"Or how would you like a life in the fantastic and fabulous corridors—lowest level—of the Empire State Building?"

"Have you gone crazy?" asked Harry.

"Very nearly," said Tucker.

Harry sighed. "And I thought I'd found you happiness."

"Happiness is fine," said Tucker. "But I've got to have some *action*, too. I mean—apart from baby carriages and flowers that never cease to bloom."

Harry lay down, and didn't purr—he sort of moaned. "Docks, skyscrapers—what do you want?"

"I want life, excitement!" shouted Tucker.

"Oh, excitement, life," mused Harry Kitten. "Where is it?"

And then his eyes changed. A glitter, an almost challenging glitter, came into them.

"Harry, stop that," said Tucker. "You don't need to go goofy—"

"Mmm," Harry purred. "Yes, life. And I *know* where it is."

"Where?" squeaked Tucker, who was sounding more like a kitten himself now.

"Times Square!" shouted Harry, although his voice cracked. "The crossroads of the whole city!"

"I'm not sure I'm up to that," whimpered Tucker.

"You'd better be," commanded this little furry kitten, Harry Kitten, who sounded now more like Harry Cat.

"Is it dangerous?" asked Tucker Mouse, wringing his paws again.

"You bet," said Harry Cat.

"Tell me about it," pleaded Tucker Mouse.

"In the very center of the very greatest city, in the very greatest country there is—there is—Times Square! The Heart of the World!"

"Harry, you are frightening me."

"There are subways—trains that run underground—there are candy stores, and hamburger joints—and most of all, there are hurrying, rushing human beings."

"I'm not so keen on them," said Tucker.

"Don't worry—they won't even notice you."

"Well, a little bit of notice," said Tucker, "would not be *too* offensive."

"And there are—I know this, because when I prowled Times Square, I saw pipes and I saw niches, and I saw places to hide."

"But the people, Harry—the human beings—you don't think they'd hound us out?"

Harry shook his head. "They're too much concerned with themselves. If we just keep out of the way of all the life that goes on there."

"Keeping out of the way of life," said Tucker. "Is that a way of life?"

Harry started to laugh. But quickly he stopped. For he saw that some moisture was dribbling down Tucker's furry cheeks.

"We have no place to live," moaned Tucker in a choked voice. "And nobody wants us."

"Now, just a minute!" Harry laid a paw on his small friend's back. "In the first place, we want each other—so

that takes care of that. And in the second, you will like
Times Square."

"Well, Harry, if you do—I might like it, too." Tucker's
whiskers—very small—were absolutely dripping now.

A curious thing then took place: a kitten wiped a
mouse's eyes. Neither one said a word. And the brush
of those paws across those wet cheeks was the strangest
touch, the most wonderful in all the world.

"Shall we give it a try?" asked Harry quietly.

"I guess so." Tucker sniffed a little. "If you say so, Harry."

And again there began the scuttle and struggle through the streets of New York. It was raining now, too. The kind of dull drizzle that everyone hates. Gray light hushed all the harsh silhouettes of the dangerous city.

But that was fortunate, on this special day. For a gray mouse and a kitten whose fur hadn't quite decided its color could pass almost unseen through the equally gray streets of the city.

The people in Times Square—when Tucker and Harry reached it, safe—were far too busy avoiding the drizzle to notice two shivering little creatures.

"We're in luck," whispered Harry.

"So this is luck," mused Tucker Mouse, as a man with a blaring radio passed by. "That penny must be a bust."

Although he could remember Tenth Avenue, Tucker had always avoided Times Square. That is, when he could: when the sanitation workers hadn't chased him in that direction. There was too much hustling and bustling there, too much pushing and shoving—and no niceness at all.

There were people dashing everywhere, and bumping each other, and not caring a bit. They all were trying desperately to escape the drizzle, which had now turned to rain.

"I know there's a grille in the street here—that leads down to the subway—" said Harry.

"The subway—" wailed Tucker.

"You'd rather get soaked in the rain? And maybe bonked by a portable radio?"

"The subway," said Tucker, utterly defeated. "And how, might I ask, do you know about the subway?"

"When I was a kitten—"

"Mmm! A lion already!"

"—I did some prowling late at night—and I'm *sure* that there's a grate near here." Harry's eyes flashed left, right —everywhere.

"And what is so safe"—Tucker Mouse was shivering —"about the subway?"

"It's *dry*, and it's *warm*. Now *will you hush up?*"

"Two very good reasons." Tucker wiggled his growing whiskers.

"There it is!" shouted Harry. "Over there! Across the street. That grille in the sidewalk."

"What eyes you have!"

"Come on. But wait for the light—"

In the very small time it takes for a traffic light to change, a mouse and a cat had dashed across Forty-second Street and vanished through a grille in the concrete.

They were just small enough to fit. And then they were gone . . .

Gone underground—to the strange, but lively, warren of the Times Square subway station.

"Isn't it wonderful!" said Harry, awe-struck. He gazed at the stores—for some of the subway stations in New York have stores in them—and at the lunch counters and newspaper stands. But "Oh, those neon lights!"—red, green, blue, a rainbow of colors—they were what fascinated him most.

"I'm scared," said Tucker, who wasn't quite so

fascinated. "I've never been in a place like this before."

"It's *marvelous*!"

"Sure, marvelous. So where do we live?"

"That remains to be seen. Discovered, I mean. I know the way in, but—"

"*But?*"

"—I don't know the layout. Let's explore."

"I've heard *that* before!" said Tucker Mouse.

But exploring they went, late at night, after hiding behind a trash can which most of the humans didn't bother to use—and when most of the commuters had pushed and crammed their way into the subway cars, to get home.

The station was more quiet then: they could do a little prowling in safety.

Harry was still bewitched by the place, and Tucker had begun to be a little bit bewitched himself—especially by the smells that came from the lunch counters. They made his mouth water.

"I might be happy here, Harry, after all," the mouse admitted breezily.

"So might we both," said Harry. "But we've got to find a place of our own. A private place."

"Like a home, you mean?"

"Exactly. A home."

It got late. And then later. The people riding the subway grew fewer and fewer. Theatergoers, mostly, yawning their long way home.

And still no special place for a kitten and a mouse.

"Let's go over near the Shuttle," said Harry.

"What's that?"

"I think it's just a little short train that goes from Times Square to some place near."

Beside the Shuttle tracks there was a kind of run-down newsstand, all boarded up for the night. But it had a friendly look.

"We could get in there," said Tucker. "Take a look at the cracks in those boards."

"Whoever owns it will open up in the morning—then what?"

Tucker sat on his haunches and sighed. "So the Times Square subway station—another no-place to live."

But Harry, whose eyes were sharper than Tucker's, had been glancing through the gloom. He thought he saw—was it?—yes, it was!—a black opening in the wall.

"There's a hole over there."

"Big deal! A hole."

"Come on—let's look."

The hole was big. And filthy.

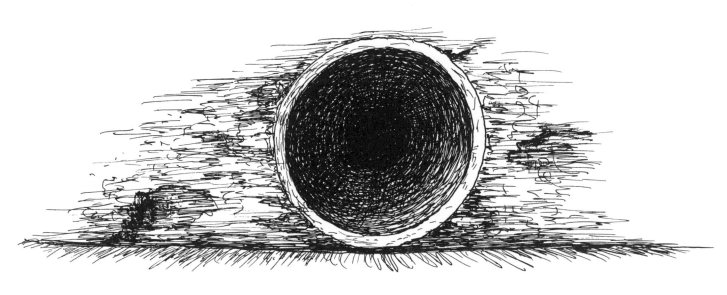

"*Yeck!* What a mess," said Tucker.

"It could be cleaned. And also—I don't think too many people know about this hole. It's a very neglected hole."

"And it smells. It's moldy, Harry—"

"*Shhh—*"

"Why shhh? There's nobody here. And no one would want to be."

"I said 'shh!' " Harry ordered.

Then Tucker heard it, too. There was a faint splashing, somewhere in back.

"A leak, too—"

"Shhh!"

Harry crept to the back of the hole. And even in the dim light that filtered in from the subway, he could see that a trickle of water was falling.

"It's *clean!*" he exclaimed. "Come take a bath!"

"I don't want a bath."

"You need a bath. And this water—it must be a leak from a copper pipe. Clean water, in a subway hole—a true miracle. Now, come on in here, and we'll get clean, too."

Tucker sputtered, and Harry laughed, and in a few minutes, after all their wandering through New York, the dirt they'd collected—inevitable, for vagabonds—had all been washed away.

They let the drifting air dry them off. And the air wasn't dirty, either. It filtered in, very softly, through the opening of the hole.

Many minutes went by.

Then Harry said, "Tucker Mouse, this is our home." He heaved the biggest sigh that has ever been heard from a growing kitten.

"It'll take a lot of cleaning—"

"Oh, Tucker," Harry said, "we're *here*! At last."

"Well, maybe it'll feel more like home when we spruce it up a little."

"It feels pretty good to me already."

"And also when I get my collection."

Harry's eyes widened. "*What* collection?"

"Oh, I don't have it yet," said Tucker airily. "But I intend to form a collection."

"A collection of what?"

"Why—why—of everything! And I'll start with my penny, the one I left back on Tenth Avenue."

"Do you mean to tell me"—Harry's fur prickled—

"that you're going to go all the way back to Tenth Avenue to retrieve one penny?"

"I am, indeed!" said Tucker. "This is one mouse that knows the value of a cent. And besides, it may have been the luck in that penny that found us this place."

"I'm living with a crazy mouse." Harry shook his head. "If you can get all the way to Tenth Avenue, and then back here again, safely—it won't be luck. It'll be another miracle!"

"So you have your miracle with running clean water, and I'll have mine with pennies." He grinned, as a new thought crossed his mind. "And maybe also nickels and dimes. And many other delightful things. But we have to clean this place out first. No collection of mine shall be housed in a dump!"

"To work, then," said Harry.

"To work," said Tucker.

If they had been men, they'd have rolled up their sleeves. But you can't roll up fur that's growing on you—so they just went to work.

And that work took many days—or rather, many nights. For they found it much safer to work at night, when the subway was almost deserted. They threw out chips and chunks of plaster, little bits of concrete, and also the leftover human trash, like a rotten banana peel, that had somehow found its way into the hole.

"You know," said Harry, when they were resting, exhausted, one night, "I think this was a drainpipe once, that got all stuck up. Do you see those watermarks there?"

"Let's hope that we don't clean it out so well that a flood comes crashing down from the street."

"Oh, we won't," said Harry. "It's stopped up for good. Except for my delightful shower. That comes from a different set of pipes, I'm sure."

"And speaking of delightful things," said Tucker, "tomorrow I go for my penny."

Harry sighed. "All right—if we must."

"Not *we. I.*"

"Tucker, I will not let you go alone. I may still be a kitten, but I'm almost a cat, and—"

"Harry," said Tucker, mouse-proud, "I, too, am growing up. And this deed I must do alone."

Harry narrowed his eyes and looked at his friend. And what he saw quite silenced him. He looked away. "If you must."

"I must."

The next night, a new moon hung in the sky—hung high above the skyscrapers of New York. It seemed like a little silver grin.

Tucker and Harry came up to the sidewalk. By now they knew many secret ways there. A sweet wind from the west had swept the city clean.

"You're really going to do it?" asked Harry.

"I really am," said Tucker. "So long. Be back in a flash!"

And the mouse was gone. Harry strained to get a last glimpse of him. Nothing.

The kitten, who *felt* like a kitten now, alone and lonely, went into their home. "Their" home? he wondered. Or was it only his. His alone. He curled and uncurled a dozen times. But sleep would not come.

Late travelers hurried by. And they, too, most of them, looked worried—as if they also had problems that might not be resolved.

Poor human beings—poor animals, thought Harry, sighing.

A young man dropped a token—and then couldn't find it. He said some very nasty words.

But Harry saw where it had landed. He rushed out and pushed the token right next to the young man's feet.

"Hey, wow!" the man shouted. "You are some cat!" He was wearing a fuzzy blue beret. "Thanks, catkins."

But Harry had hurried back to his home.

Where he waited.

And waited...

And *waited*! ... And along with his waiting, his worry grew heavier and heavier.

Until a *plink* sounded in the drainpipe.

"Here's the penny!"

"You *found* it? And got *back*—"

"I think it should be"—Tucker glanced around—"above the mantelpiece!" Just casually he threw in: "I *did* have trouble with that sanitation truck. Those big wheels, you know. Ah, well—I do think the mantelpiece. Except we have no mantelpiece." His eyes wandered here and there. "How about above the entrance to the drainpipe?"

"Great!" Harry looked away and blinked. "Just great. You put it there, though. It's yours."

"It is ours," said Tucker. He placed the penny carefully on a little ledge of stone that stood out above the drainpipe opening. "There. Now, that's a beginning."

And indeed a beginning it was!

For now Tucker Mouse truly knew that collecting things—"scrounging," he called it—was his vocation. (And vocation is what human beings call their life's work.)

He was very lucky, Tucker was, in small change. Apart from pennies, he found a few nickels—and on one glorious afternoon, a quarter.

"The bliss of it," he crooned.

But as well as cash, he also found funny human things. Like a lady's crazy hat: droopy and blue, with a vivid pink feather.

"Will you look at that!"

"I'm looking," said Harry. "It's very ordinary."

"Ordinary is nice," said Tucker Mouse.

And all the time that Tucker Mouse had been collecting—"scrounging"—Harry had been slinking and watching and observing the subway station. And wisely, he observed it all.

He'd observed that there was one man with a red necktie who always made his train if he wore that red necktie. And if he didn't wear it—he lost: the doors closed on his face. His luck is in his necktie, Harry thought. Maybe.

Harry Cat observed a lot. And thought and thought.

"So what are you looking so gloomy for?" asked
Tucker one night. He was especially happy that night.
He'd found two dimes.

"There are others living here, besides us two," said
Harry Cat. "And if you don't believe me, just look across
the tracks."

Tucker looked. Six eyes—two by two—were staring at
them.

"Who *are* they?"

"*Rats!* And worse than those miserable creatures we
met on the docks."

"Rats—"

"And they're big! They live in garbage cans. And
they're looking at us."

"Just jealous," said Tucker.

"Maybe," said Harry. "But I want to grow big—very fast. You've been so busy collecting, you haven't seen the eyes. Just look at them!"

Across the subway tracks, those eyes of three rats—steely-greedy—all stared at Tucker and Harry.

"And garbage cans! Who would live there—?"

"Someone hungry"—Tucker tried to make the best of it—"who has no place else to live. You and I weren't doing so well ourselves for a while."

"We never stooped to garbage cans."

Harry grumbled in his throat. "I just don't like the look of those *eyes*. I like the man with the red necktie, and I like the lady who only wears sneakers, but I don't like those eyes. They've been staring at us for *days* now."

"They have?"

"I'll say! And those guys are big, too!"

"Well, you keep an eye on those eyes," said Tucker. "I'm sure it'll be all right."

"Mmm—I wonder," said Harry.

And secretly, although he put on a brave face, Tucker, too, began to worry. He had grown so fond of his collection: the buttons and bits of ribbon, not to mention the money. The thought of anyone preying on them made his fur bristle.

In the course of the next few days, Tucker's worry grew and grew.

He finally had to talk about it. "Harry," he said one

night, "you don't think those rats would—would *steal* anything from my collection—"

"They might."

"But *why?* I only collect the things I like. And even the money. I just like to look at those lovely dimes."

"And sometimes roll around in them."

"So who is harmed if every now and then I take a nickel rinse. But rats don't like beautiful things. What *good* would they be to them, anyway."

"I'll give you an example," said Harry. "You remember what you found yesterday?"

Tucker sighed. "Just costume jewelry—but gorgeous!"

"Yes. Well, a rat could steal that pin and drop it in one of the lunch counters. And while the waitresses were fighting over who found it first, he could eat up a pound of hamburger."

"Oh, dear!" Tucker wrung his front paws. "They would *use* my treasures—"

"You bet they would. Because rats *are* users. And they have no sense of beauty at all."

Now Tucker's worry turned to panic. He was so panic-stricken that he almost stopped collecting completely. But not if an especially choice item—like a lady's hairpin —just happened to fall outside the drainpipe opening.

The days wore on . . .

The six eyes stared . . .

And Tucker Mouse thought he just might lose his mouse mind.

But even he had to sleep sometimes. He woke up one night—it was very late—and saw Harry staring out into the subway. "Is something wrong?" He jumped to his feet.

"I thought I heard something."

Tucker Mouse did not have time to ask what.

The raid was upon them . . .

However, it didn't feel like a raid at first.

"Hi, guys!" said the biggest rat. "I t'ought we'z oughta get acquainted."

67

"Oh, delighted to," said Harry Cat, and flashed a warning glance at Tucker.

The strangest thing about these rats was, they all looked alike. One was huge, and one was middle-sized, and one might be called little—although he was at least twice as big as Tucker Mouse. Their fur was a kind of dirty gray—and there *was* dirt on it—but their eyes—oh, their eyes!—were identical: sharp, fierce, piercing, and full of malice.

"I'm Chollie," said the biggest rat.

"I assume that means Charlie," said Harry Cat.

"Yeah, Chollie means Chollie," said Chollie Rat. "An' dis is Spud"—he pointed a claw at the middle-sized rat—"so called cuz potatoes is his favorite food. An' da runt is the Bump. Fa da reason dat looms at da end of his nose."

The Bump had a nervous laugh—if one could call it a laugh. It was more like a high, queer shriek. "Yeah, the Bump. I'm the Bump." He squealed with delight.

"I wish you wouldn't do that," said Tucker. "It's very upsetting."

"So, upset," said the Bump. "We all got our problems." His mad laughter fluttered insanely, again.

"I am not happy, Harry," Tucker said to his friend.

"Why?" said Chollie. "It's just a frien'ly call."

"Yeah, so's us guys can get to know youse guys," said Spud.

Tucker shot Harry a very nervous look. "In fact, I am very *un*happy, Harry."

"You notice how nice da little mouse smells?" said Chollie to Spud.

"I took a shower before retiring tonight," said Tucker. "It's a practice I strongly urge all you three to adopt."

This remark brought forth the wildest giggling yet from the Bump.

By now, inch by inch, the rats had edged their way into the drainpipe. Tucker and Harry found themselves backed against one wall.

"So—a mouse an' a kitten livin' togetha," said Chollie. "A very strange combination."

"I am *not* a kitten," said Harry, with as much conviction as he could. "I'm a *cat*."

"Youse still are a kitten—with a kitten's little whiskers." Chollie flicked Harry's whiskers with one claw. Then he flicked his own. "Whereas dese are da whiskas of a full-grown rat!"

"Well, it's been nice to meet you," squeaked Tucker. "If there's ever anything you should need—like a shower—"

"Need—" said Chollie, and a glint of teeth appeared behind an evil smile. "We don't *need* nothin'. But there's somethin' we *want*." The sound that came from his mouth was part snarl, part growl, and part hiss. "We want what we been seein' you rake in dis hole, my little freaky-furry friend. An' we're gonna get it! So don't fight

—don't argue—just hand over all you got!"

"My Life Savings—" shrieked Tucker.

"If dat's what you call da loot—yeah! Ya life's savin's."

"I will not!" And shivering though he was—a bit from the dampness still in his fur, since he hadn't dried himself too well earlier—Tucker Mouse stamped his foot. "No! Never!"

"Yeah, ya will," said Chollie, in a quiet, deadly kind of voice—as if bored, as if the whole awful transaction had already been completed. "Or else I'll hoit ya very bad. An' den take da stuff anyway."

At that, Harry Cat blew up. "I told you," he shouted at Tucker. "These are *bums*. They'd plant a dime just to bite someone's leg who was picking it up."

"Not a bad idea," chuckled Chollie Rat. "Da kitty's got a sense of humor. An' by da way, we'll be back every month to collect what youse have picked up in da meantime."

"No—" Now Harry, too, spoke quietly, although his voice broke a little, since Chollie was right: he wasn't a cat yet. "No, you will not. You will not take one item of my friend's possessions. And furthermore, you will leave these premises which are our home—right now!— and go back to whichever filthy garbage can you call *your* home."

For a moment Chollie Rat just stared at this dopey little kitten, whose fur was still fuzzy, and who had challenged him, given *him*, Chollie Rat, an order to go.

71

But for only a moment did Chollie Rat stare.

Then he lunged at Harry and sank his hideous sharp teeth in the kitten's shoulder. Harry screamed—as a cat can scream, not simply yowl—for the pain was horrible.

But Tucker didn't scream—he roared! A real roar for a very small mouse. Then he went for Chollie, and bit his tail.

"Ow! *Ow!*" And the rat let go of Harry. Tucker bit in deeper.

Chollie bared all his teeth. And Tucker knew that, for him at least, the fight was over. He might as well be dead.

But he wasn't dead. Because, once those fangs were out of his shoulder, Harry jumped on Chollie's back and started clawing, as best he could with claws that weren't yet grown.

Meanwhile, the two other rats had been gawking. They couldn't believe that a kitten and a mouse would fight back—and particularly at their boss, Chollie Rat. But now they knew they had to join the battle, too. They had to help Chollie, because if they didn't, he'd skin them alive.

A frenzy—a frantic and furious chaos—of claws, paws, teeth, tails, now occurred. No one was winning.

But suddenly Chollie Rat shouted, *"Hold it!"*

In the fury—the fighting—the scratching and biting—the whole situation had ended like this: Harry Kitten, who now was definitely Harry Cat, had managed to flatten Chollie. The rat lay on his back, and Harry sprawled over him. And Tucker Mouse, with the tiny instinct that small persecuted people have, had raised one small but very sharp claw above Chollie's tender nose.

"Stop! Stop!" shouted Chollie. "Oo! Oo! My nose—"

"You better stop," Tucker said. For a mouse he suddenly felt very strong. "And you'd better tell your friends to go home. Otherwise—" It was horrible—but—to save their home— "Otherwise, I'm going to claw a good gouge from your nose." And he only hoped that his claws were big enough to carry out his threat.

"Go on, you guys!" whimpered Chollie Rat. He didn't sound one single bit like his former bragging and blustering self. "Go on! Back to da gahbitch can. My nose—! Ooo—"

"Oh, wow!" said the Bump, who hadn't said a single word till then. "An' I t'ought *I* was da cowahd." He tittered again.

The Bump and Spud backed out of the drainpipe.

Very gingerly, Harry and Tucker let Chollie go. And he went *fast*!—out of shame as well as pain.

Neither mouse nor cat had the strength to speak. For at least five minutes there was only relief—peace.

"He said they'd be back in a month," Tucker Mouse finally found the breath to say.

"Now, don't worry!" Harry Cat had long since realized that the best way, the only way, to quiet his friend was to flatten him gently on the floor with a paw, claws in. "With all the lunch stands here, I'll be able to eat a lot. And in one month"—he reared up on his hind legs and showed off his growing muscles—"in just one month, I'll be so big that all the rats in New York will tremble. Most of all, those hooligans!"

"Very impressive, I must say," said Tucker, who knew

that for the rest of his life he would always be a mouse.

"And by the way"—Harry tapped Tucker's head—"Mousiekins, you saved my life. By biting that nasty creature's tail."

"Yes, and you saved my Life Savings," said Tucker.

Harry Cat had to laugh at that. And it wasn't just the purring murmur of a cat's delight. It was more like the howling yowling of mirth. And happiness. And safety. And home. "And of course they are equally important. My life—and your life savings, that is."

"Oh, Harry, I didn't mean—"

But Tucker was abruptly distracted. A splash of silver fell at his feet.

"Come on, Master Mouse! I was only kidding—"

"Look, Harry."

At a certain hour of the night a ray of moonlight, if the moon was full, fell through a grating, above, in Times Square. And fell like a silent poem—a prayer—in front of the drainpipe where Harry and Tucker now lived.

They both looked at the silvery light. And then they went out, to get the feel of it on their backs.

The moonlight made the fur of both animals shine. It felt as if it were shining inside them, too.

Tucker Mouse was silent. And then he coughed. The late stillness of the subway station—so beautiful and difficult—just had to be broken.

And then it was really broken—harshly: a clattering train rushed in.

One man ran to catch it. And made it.

A lady cried, "Oh, please wait!" The man firmly held the door open for her. "Oh, thank you," she said. The train sped away.

"I'm glad she caught it," murmured Tucker. But Harry said nothing. He shone.